Top
=secrets=
by

Jenni makes monkey faces at me while Im trying to do my work 3 times a day. That equals 15 in one week

Allison fell asleep in class every day this week
monday + tuesday + wednes + thursday + frida = 5 times in one week!

Emma J tells o e too in clas 43 times every nth.

# The Great Math Tattle Battle

**Anne Bowen**          **Illustrated by Jaime Zollars**

Erin talks all the time during class: 4 times on monday 2 times on Wednesday and 1 time on Friday 4 + 2 + 1 = ⑦ = times in ONE WEEK!

Blah Blah blah

① 10 + ② 10 + ③ 10 = 30 times every single week. 10 boys at recess strike out the game. 3 games per week. that's 10 times in every

Kristin S.

Eric Z. asks too many questions in class. 4 every single day of the week.
4 + 4 + 4 + 4 + 4 = 20
4 + 4 = 8 + 4 = 12 + 4 = 16 + 4 = 20

Megan does cartwheels in the hallway when the teachers aren't looking so many times I can't even count.

For Taylor, Addison, Mathew, and Aden.—AB

To Mom and Dad, who bought me my first sketchbook and encouraged me to draw.—JZ

Harley Harrison was the best math student in second grade.

He could figure out forty-five plus thirty-nine faster than you could spell "Mississippi."

He could count to one hundred by any number.
Twos, fives, twenties. It didn't matter. Math was a piece
of cake for Harley.

Harley was also the biggest
tattletale in second grade.
Nothing escaped his blue
spiral notebook . . .

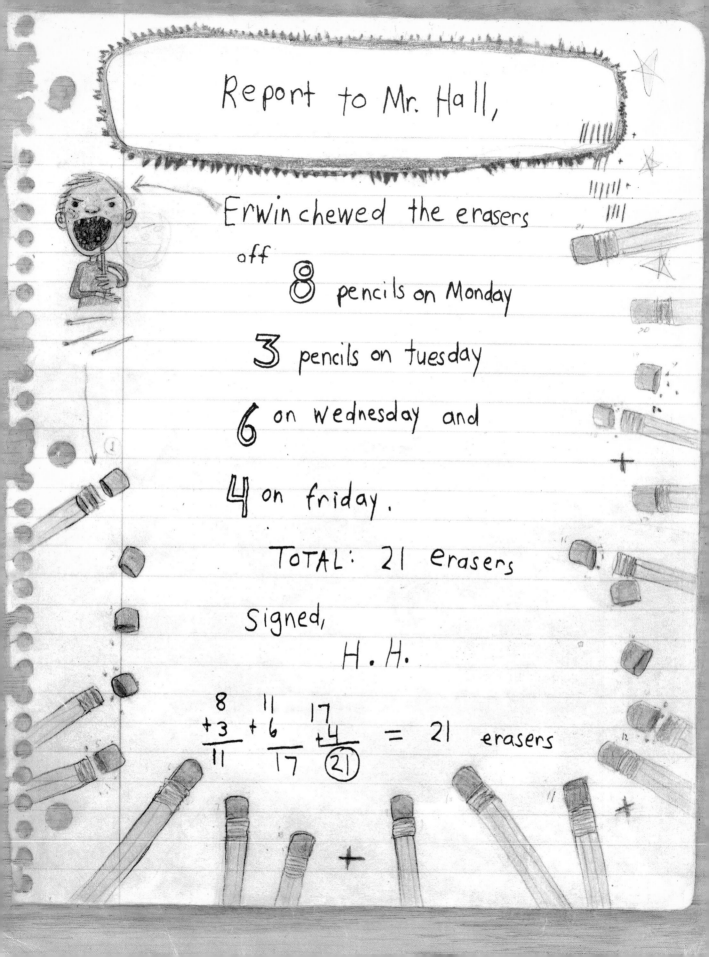

Report to Mr. Hall,

Erwin chewed the erasers off

8 pencils on Monday

3 pencils on tuesday

6 on wednesday and

4 on friday.

TOTAL: 21 erasers

Signed,
H. H.

$$\frac{8}{+3} + \frac{11}{17} \quad \frac{17}{21} = 21 \text{ erasers}$$

"You are a big, fat tattletale, Harley Harrison," said Erwin. "No wonder no one wants to be your math partner."

"You might choke on those erasers," replied Harley.

"Harley, this is none of your business," said Mr. Hall, the second-grade teacher.

When the Swanson twins forgot to clean up under their desks, Harley was on the spot with his notebook:

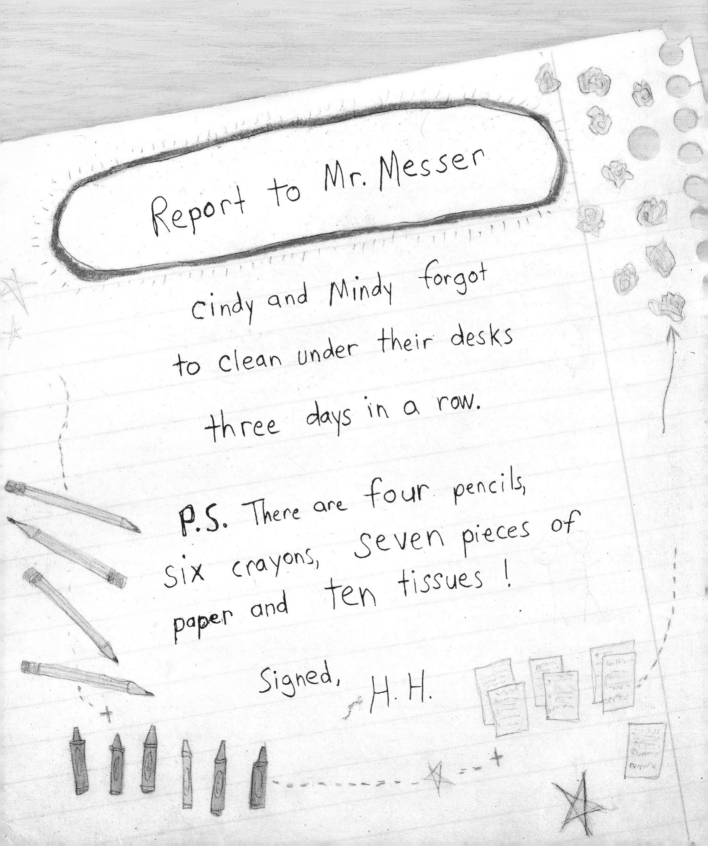

Report to Mr. Messer

Cindy and Mindy forgot to clean under their desks three days in a row.

P.S. There are four pencils, six crayons, seven pieces of paper and ten tissues!

Signed,
H. H.

"You are such a big tattletale, Harley Harrison," said Cindy and Mindy. "No wonder no one wants to help you with your art project."

"You could get germs from a mess like that," replied Harley.

"Please mind your own business," said Mr. Messer, the custodian.

But that didn't stop Harley.

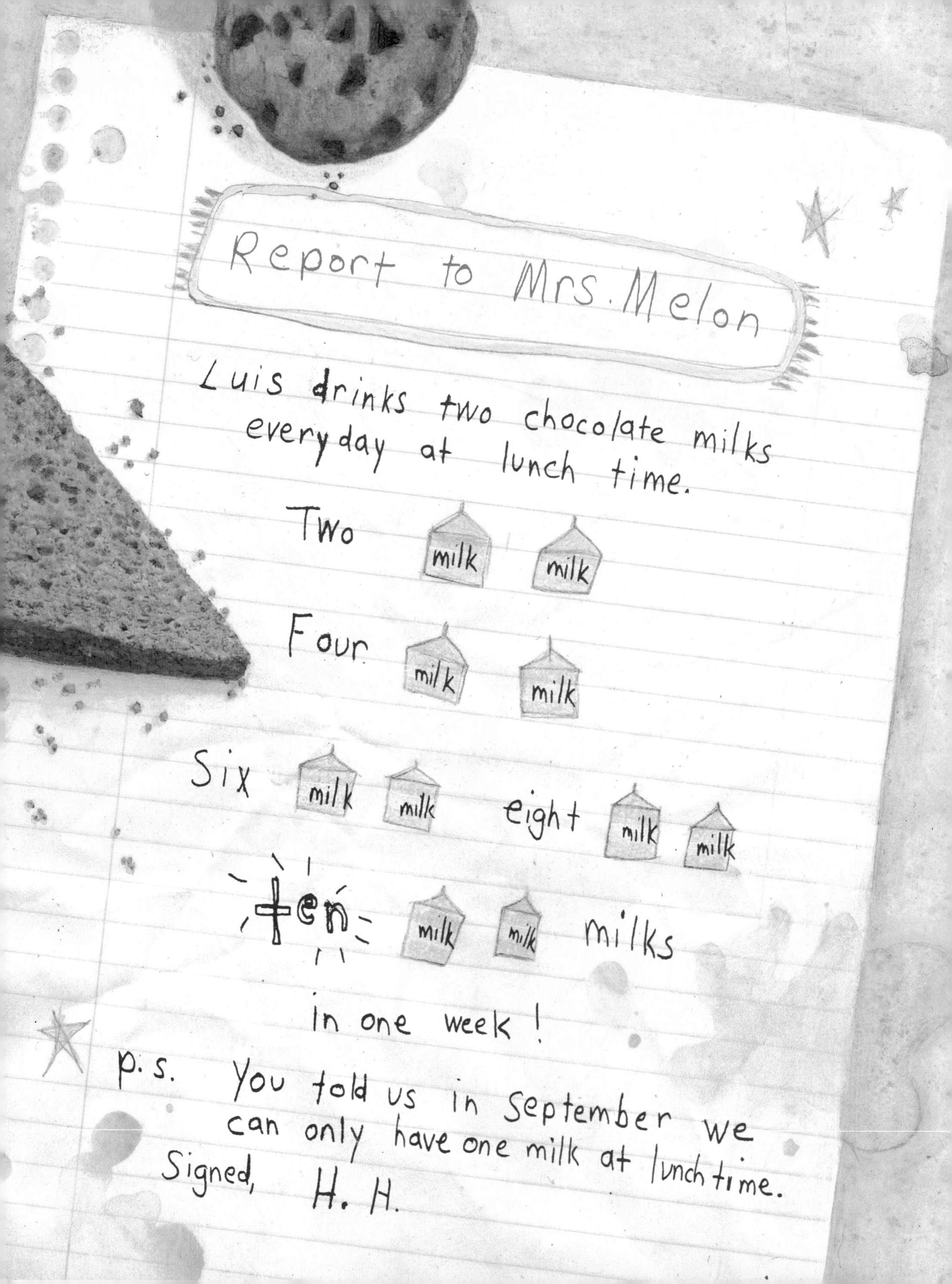

Report to Mrs. Melon

Luis drinks two chocolate milks everyday at lunch time.

Two milk milk

Four milk milk

Six milk milk eight milk milk

ten milk milk milks

in one week!

p.s. You told us in September we can only have one milk at lunch time.

Signed, H. H.

"It's the BIG TATTLETALE again," said Luis. "No wonder you eat lunch all by yourself."

"You could get cavities from so much sugar," replied Harley.

"Harley, I can take care of this," said Mrs. Melon, the lunch lady.

One Monday morning in the middle of math, a new student marched into class.

"My name is Emma Jean Smith," she announced.

"Welcome, Emma Jean. You can sit in the empty desk next to Harley Harrison," said Mr. Hall.

Harley was too busy adding and subtracting to notice.

Emma Jean leaned over and looked at Harley's math paper.

"Thirty-five plus sixty-four equals ninety-nine," said Emma Jean.

"And the next answer is fifty-six," she told Harley.

"And that one is seventy-nine," Emma Jean said. "It's a good thing I helped you with those problems or they would be all wrong."

Harley couldn't believe his ears.

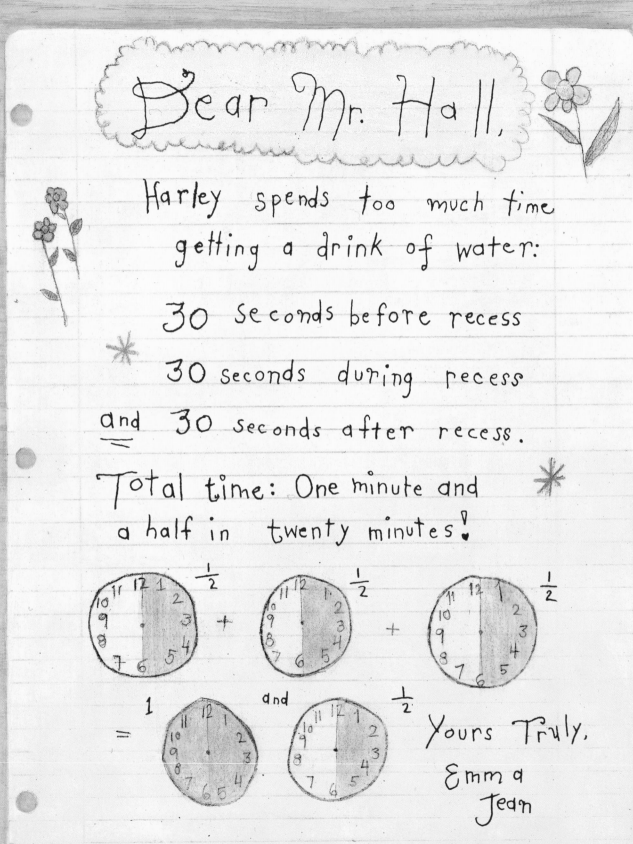

Harley couldn't believe his eyes.
"You're a tattletale, Emma Jean,"
said Harley.
"You're wasting everyone's
time at the water fountain," replied
Emma Jean.
Mr. Hall wasn't sure what to say.

After library, Harley handed Mr. Hall a page of his blue spiral notebook.

☆ Report to Mr. Hall,
    Emma Jean whispered five times in twenty minutes in the library. That's one whisper every four minutes.
    Signed, H.H.

During writing time, Emma Jean scribbled a note to Mr. Hall.

Dear

Mr. Hall,

Harley sharpened his pencil

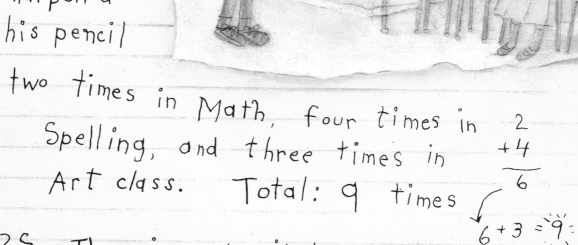

two times in Math, four times in Spelling, and three times in Art class.   Total: 9 times

$2$
$+4$
___
$6$

$6 + 3 = 9$

P.S. The noise makes it difficult to concentrate on our learning.

Yours truly, Emma Jean

On Thursday during math, Mr. Hall said to the class, "Today, I want you to pair up with the person sitting next to you. You will have thirty minutes to answer the problems. Those partners who finish all the problems and get 100 percent may have an extra ten minutes at recess for the next four days."

Emma Jean said, "I can
do these myself."
"Me, too," said Harley.
"Piece of cake."

They started adding and subtracting faster than you could spell "Alabama."

Harley glanced at Emma Jean and noticed she was frowning. He leaned over. "The answer is one hundred and two," said Harley.

"I knew that," said Emma Jean. She looked at the
next problem on Harley's paper. "That one's easy. The
answer is seventy-two."

"You forgot to write four in the tens place," said Harley.
"And you made a mistake right there." Emma Jean pointed.
"And you said you were going to work by yourself," said Harley.
"And so did you!" said Emma Jean.

# MATH CHALLENGE

Name: Harley Harrison

$$
\begin{array}{r} 32 \\ +40 \\ \hline 72 \end{array}
\qquad
\begin{array}{r} \overset{1}{6}1 \\ +49 \\ \hline 110 \end{array}
\qquad
\begin{array}{r} 82 \\ +67 \\ \hline 149 \end{array}
\qquad
\begin{array}{r} \overset{1}{6}7 \\ +67 \\ \hline \cancel{124} \end{array}
\qquad
\begin{array}{r} 71 \\ +48 \\ \hline 119 \end{array}
$$

$$
\begin{array}{r} \overset{1}{7}6 \\ +89 \\ \hline 165 \end{array}
\qquad
\begin{array}{r} \overset{1}{9}9 \\ +99 \\ \hline 19\cancel{8}8 \end{array}
\qquad
\begin{array}{r} \overset{1}{3}6 \\ +85 \\ \hline 121 \end{array}
\qquad
\begin{array}{r} 33 \\ +30 \\ \hline 43 \end{array}
\qquad
\begin{array}{r} \overset{1}{4}4 \\ +28 \\ \hline 72 \end{array}
$$

$$
\begin{array}{r} 62 \\ +81 \\ \hline \end{array}
\qquad
\begin{array}{r} 49 \\ +22 \\ \hline \end{array}
\qquad
\begin{array}{r} 89 \\ +45 \\ \hline 134 \end{array}
\qquad
\begin{array}{r} 22 \\ +80 \\ \hline \end{array}
\qquad
\begin{array}{r} \\ + \\ \hline \end{array}
$$

When Mr. Hall said, "Only ten minutes left," they both jumped in their chairs. It didn't take a math whiz to notice everyone else was almost finished. Harley and Emma Jean still had the other side of the paper to do!

"Uh-oh," said Harley. "Only ten minutes left!"

"And twenty problems," said Emma Jean.

"Listen," said Harley. "If you do the next ten problems—"

"And you do the last ten," said Emma Jean. "We can finish in time."

And that's just what they did. Faster than you can spell "Massachusetts."

Friday afternoon, Mr. Hall found another note on his desk . . .

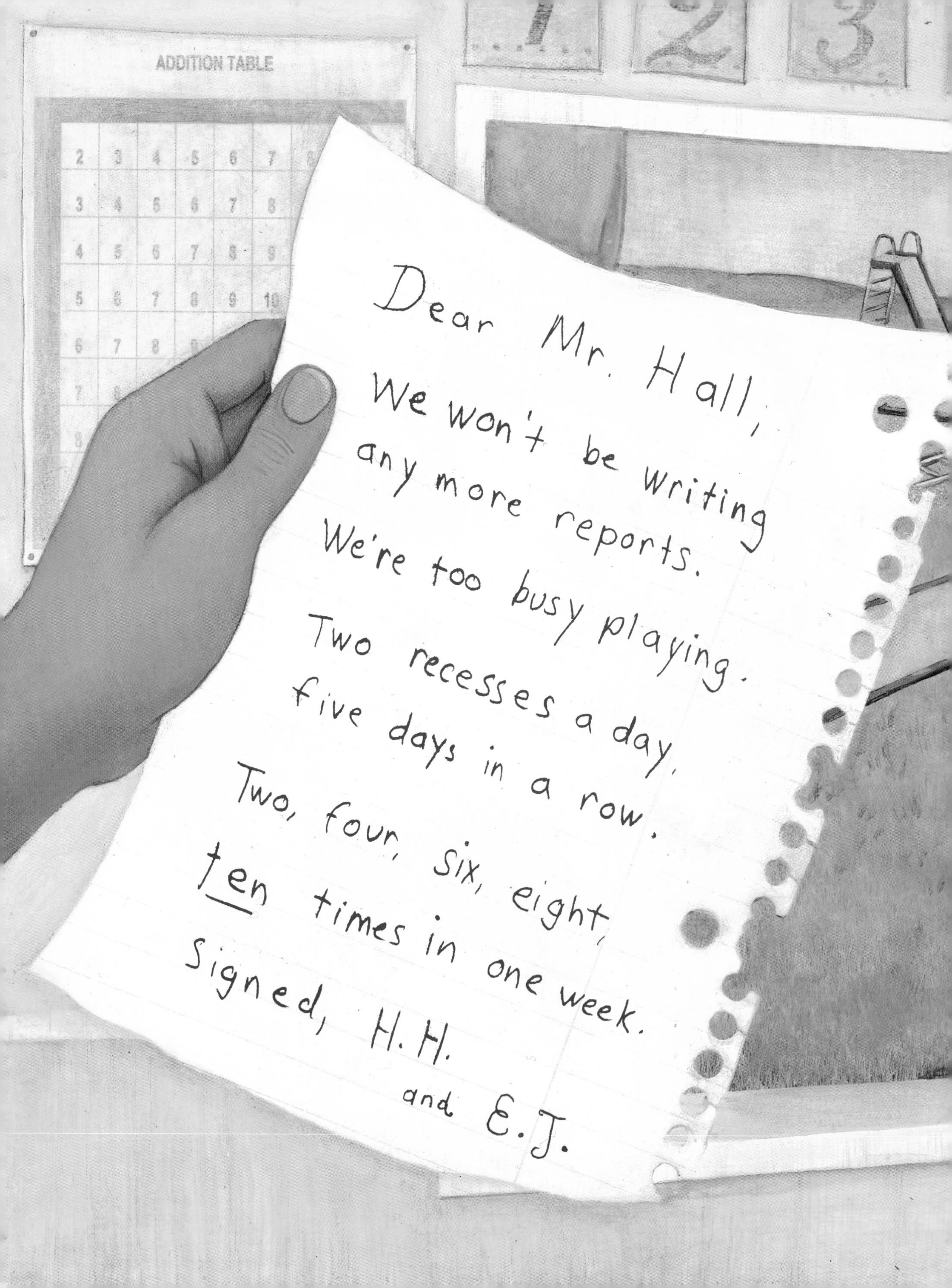
ADDITION TABLE
Dear Mr. Hall,
We won't be writing
any more reports.
We're too busy playing.
Two recesses a day,
five days in a row.
Two, four, six, eight,
ten times in one week.
Signed, H.H.
and E.J.

**1.** There are **110** students in Harley and Emma Jean's grade at school. **83** of them like math. (Hurray for them!) How many students don't like math?

**2.** Luis drinks **10** milks every week at lunch. How many milks does he drink in **4** weeks? **8** weeks? **10** weeks?

**3.** **50** pencils come in a box. How many pencils are left in the box after Erwin chewed **21** of them?

**4.** If Emma Jean whispers to her friends **5** times every **20** minutes, how many times does she whisper to her friends in one hour?

**5.** Remember when Harley tattled on Cindy and Mindy Swanson for not cleaning up under their desks? How many pieces of trash did the twins leave on the floor? (Hint: go back and read Harley's note to Mr. Messer!)

# Battle Teasers

**6.** On Monday, Harley did **10** addition problems. On Tuesday, he did **13**. On Wednesday, he did **15**. On Thursday, he was home sick and didn't do any problems! But on Friday, he did **11**.

On Monday, Emma Jean did **9** addition problems. On Tuesday, she did **14**. On Wednesday, she was late to school (she brought a note!) and missed math class. But on Thursday, she did **16**. And on Friday, she did **11**, just like Harley.

Who did the most addition problems, Harley or Emma Jean?

Turn the page for answers!

## Answers to Teasers

1. **27** students don't like math. (Too bad!)

2. Luis drinks **40** milks in four weeks, **80** milks in eight weeks, **100** milks in ten weeks! (Wow!)

3. **29** pencils are left.

4. **15** times!

5. **4** pencils + **6** crayons + **7** pieces of paper + **10** tissues = **27**! (What a mess!)

6. Harley does **49** problems. Emma Jean does **50**!

Library of Congress Cataloging-in-Publication Data

Bowen, Anne, 1952-
The great math tattle battle / by Anne Bowen ; illustrated by Jaime Zollars.
p. cm.
Summary: Harley Harrison, the biggest tattle-tale and best math student in second grade,
meets his match in both areas when Emma Jean Smith joins him Mr. Hall's class.
ISBN-13: 978-0-8075-3163-1 (hardcover)
ISBN-10: 0-8075-3163-4 (hardcover)
[1. Talebearing—Fiction. 2. Mathematics—Fiction. 3. Schools—Fiction.]
I. Zollars, Jaime, ill. II. Title.
PZ7.B671945Gre 2006  [E]—dc22  2005026192

The design is by Jaime Zollars and Carol Gildar.

For more information about Albert Whitman & Company,
visit our web site at www.albertwhitman.com.